Millions of Americans remember Dick and Jane (and Sally and Spot too!). The little stories with their simple vocabulary words and warmly rendered illustrations were a hallmark of American education in the 1950s and 1960s.

But the first Dick and Jane stories actually appeared much earlier—in the Scott Foresman Elson Basic Reader Pre-Primer, copyright 1930. These books featured short, upbeat, and highly readable stories for children. The pages were filled with colorful characters and large, easy-to-read Century Schoolbook typeface. There were fun adventures around every corner of Dick and Jane's world.

Generations of American children learned to read with Dick and Jane, and many still cherish the memory of reading the simple stories on their own. Today, Pearson Scott Foresman remains committed to helping all children learn to read—and love to read. As part of Pearson Education, the world's largest educational publisher, Pearson Scott Foresman is honored to reissue these classic Dick and Jane stories, with Grosset & Dunlap, a division of Penguin Young Readers Group. Reading has always been at the heart of everything we do, and we sincerely hope that reading is an important part of your life too.

Dick and Jane® is a registered trademark of Addison-Wesley Educational Publishers, Inc.
From THE NEW WE LOOK AND SEE. Copyright © 1956 by Scott Foresman and Company,
copyright renewed 1984. From THE NEW WE WORK AND PLAY. Copyright © 1956 by
Scott Foresman and Company, copyright renewed 1984. All rights reserved. Published by
Grosset & Dunlap, a division of Penguin Young Readers Group, 345 Hudson Street, New York,
NY, 10014. GROSSET & DUNLAP is a trademark of Penguin Group (USA) Inc.
Published simultaneously in Canada. Printed in the U.S.A.

Library of Congress Cataloging-in-Publication Data is available.

ISBN 0-448-43400-8 (pbk)   D E F G H I J
ISBN 0-448-43412-1 (GB)   D E F G H I J

Read with

Dick and Jane

We Look

GROSSET & DUNLAP • NEW YORK

Look

Look, look.

Oh, oh, oh.

Oh, oh.

Oh, look.

Jane

Oh, Jane.

Look, Jane, look.

Look, look.

Oh, look.

See Jane.

See, see.

See Jane.

Oh, see Jane.

Dick

Look, Jane.
Look, look.
See Dick.

See, see.

Oh, see.

See Dick.

Oh, see Dick.

Oh, oh, oh.

Funny, funny Dick.

Sally

Look, Dick.
Look, Jane.
See Sally.

Oh, oh, oh.

Oh, Dick.

See Sally.

Look, Jane.

Look, Dick.

See funny Sally.

Funny, funny Sally.

Big and Little

Come, come.

Come and see.

See Father and Mother.

Father is big.

Mother is little.

Look, Father.

Dick is big.

Sally is little.

Big, big Dick.

Little Baby Sally.

Oh, look, Jane.

Look, Dick, look.

Sally is big.

Tim is little.

Big, big Sally.

Little Baby Tim.

The Funny Baby

Come down, Dick.

Come and see.

See the big, big mother.

See the funny little baby.

Puff is my baby.

Puff is my funny little baby.

I see the big mother.
I see the little baby.
Look, Jane.
See the big father.

Look, Dick, look.

See something funny.

See my baby jump.

See my baby run.

Oh, oh, oh.

Something Blue

Oh, Jane, I see something.

I see something blue.

Come and see Mother work.

Mother can make something.

Something blue.

Look Mother, look.

I can work.

I can make something.

I can make something yellow.

Look, look.

See something yellow.

Oh, Jane, I can work.

I can make something blue.

I can make something yellow.

Oh, see my funny Tim.

Little Tim is yellow.

Baby Sally is blue.